TRANSFORMERS

Based on the screenplay by
Roberto Orci & Alex Kurtzman

From a story by Roberto Orci & Alex Kurtzman
and John Rogers

CB003199

LEVEL 1

Adapted by: Paul Shipton
Publisher: Jacquie Bloese
Commissioning Editor: Helen Parker
Editor: Fiona Davis
Cover layout: Christine Cox
Designer: Christine Cox
Picture Research: Emma Bree

Photo credits: Cover image and inside photos provided courtesy of Hasbro / Paramount Pictures Corporation.
Pages 4 & 5: C. Davidson/Alamy; E. Miller/Getty Images; Allstar.
Pages 13, 14, 17 & 31: Allstar.
Pages 32 & 33: WENN; Hasbro.
Pages 34 & 35: Dreamworks/Paramount/BFI; F. Harrison, F. M. Brown, B. Bedder, K. Winter/Getty Images.
Pages 36 & 37: S. Gallup, Y. Tsuno, AFP/Getty Images.

Licensed by:

HASBRO and its logo, TRANSFORMERS and all related characters are trademarks of Hasbro and are used with permission. © 2007 Hasbro. All Rights Reserved.© 2006 DreamWorks LLC and Paramount Pictures Corporation.

Copyright © 2008 by Hasbro. All rights reserved.

© 2008 Dream Works LLC and Paramount Pictures Corporation.

Camaro, Topkick and Hummer H2 © General Motors

No part of this publication may be reproduced in whole or in part, or stored in a retrieval system, or transmitted in any form or by any means, electronic, mechanical, photocopying, recording or otherwise, without written permission of the publisher. For information regarding permission write to:

Mary Glasgow Magazines (Scholastic Ltd.)
Euston House
24 Eversholt Street
London NW1 1DB

Original text and design © Scholastic Ltd 2009
All rights reserved.

Printed in Singapore

Contents

	Page
Transformers	**4–31**
People and places	**4**
Chapter 1: Under attack	**6**
Chapter 2: Frenzy	**9**
Chapter 3: The yellow robot	**12**
Chapter 4: The open door	**14**
Chapter 5: The Allspark	**18**
Chapter 6: The Ice Man	**23**
Chapter 7: The last fight	**27**
Fact Files	**32–37**
It started with a toy …	**32–33**
Transformers – the film	**34–35**
Robot world	**36–37**
Self-Study Activities	**38–40**
New Words	**inside back cover**

PEOPLE AND PLACES

TRANSFORMERS

SAM WITWICKY is a teenager and he lives with his mom and dad. Sam wants two things – a car and a girlfriend. When his dad buys him his first car, he gets a lot more than this ...

THE AUTOBOTS

are good robots from the planet Cybertron. But why are they here on Earth?

OPTIMUS PRIME is the leader of the Autobots. He can change into a big truck.

BUMBLEBEE can change into a yellow car. He can only speak through the radio.

OTHER AUTOBOTS:
Jazz
Ironhide
Ratchet

PLACES

QATAR is a hot country close to Saudi Arabia. The USA has some military bases there.

THE PENTAGON is an important US government building in Washington, DC.

MIKAELA BANES is the most beautiful girl in Sam's school. Sam is in love with her, but she doesn't know his name!

CAPTAIN LENNOX is a very good soldier. He is far from home – on a US military base in Qatar.

THE DECEPTICONS

are bad robots from the planet Cybertron. They are always attacking the Autobots.

MEGATRON is Optimus Prime's brother and the leader of the Decepticons. He is very strong. But where is Megatron now?

FRENZY is a very small robot and can change into a CD player. He's very good with computers.

OTHER DECEPTICONS:
Starscream
Barricade
Bonecrusher
Blackout

THE HOOVER DAM is between Arizona and Nevada in the USA.

MISSION CITY is a city near the Hoover Dam.

TRANSFORMERS

CHAPTER 1
Under attack

Captain Lennox and his men were at the US military base in Qatar. After many months at the base, the men wanted to see their families again.

'We're going home soon,' said Captain Lennox, and the men were happy.

But then everything changed.

'A helicopter is coming,' shouted a soldier in the computer room. 'But it isn't ours.'

The soldiers at the base were ready when the black helicopter arrived.

'Get out of the helicopter or you are going to die!' shouted one of the soldiers.

There was no answer from the helicopter. Suddenly there was a loud scream and the helicopter started to move. It changed into a giant robot. The soldiers were fightened. They started to fire, but the robot fired back. The base was under attack.

In the computer room a soldier shouted, 'Something is trying to get into our computers!'

One of Lennox's soldiers ran up close to the robot. He fired up at it. The robot started to fall.

'Run!' shouted Lennox to his men.

The soldier stopped and took a photo of the robot's big red eyes. Then he turned and ran, too. Was the robot dead? Lennox and his men didn't have time to look back. They just ran and ran.

* * *

'OK, Mr Witwicky,' said the teacher. 'You're next.'
Sam Witwicky went to the front of the class.

'I'm going to tell you about my grandfather, no sorry, my *grandfather's* grandfather, Captain Archibald Witwicky,' Sam said. 'He was a famous man. In 1897 he was one of the first Americans to go to the Arctic.' Sam emptied his school bag on the desk. 'All these things are his. Here are his glasses. They probably saw some fantastic things.' He looked up. 'I'm selling all of these things. Just look on the Internet.'

'Witwicky!' said the teacher angrily. 'This is a school, not a shop!'

'OK ... OK ...' Sam showed the class an old newspaper. 'Archibald saw a giant man in the Arctic ice!'

Some of the other students started to laugh now.

'No one believed him,' said Sam. 'When he came back, they put him in a hospital.'

It was the end of the class and students started to leave. 'Don't forget!' called Sam. 'I'm selling the glasses!'

Sam needed money because he wanted a car. After school his dad took him to look at some in a shop.

The shop owner, Bobby, put an arm around Sam. 'Listen. Your first car is special. But the driver doesn't find the car – the car finds the driver.'

Sam looked around and then walked to a yellow car. It was old but it looked fast. 'I like this one.'

'I don't remember this car,' thought Bobby. But he was still happy to sell it.

'How much?' asked Sam's dad.

'Five thousand.'

'I can't pay more than four.'

Suddenly the radio in the yellow car came on. A loud, high scream came out of the radio. SMASH! Windows in the other cars started to break. Bobby looked around, his mouth open. Then he looked at the yellow car again. He turned to Sam and his dad.

'OK … four thousand,' said Bobby.

CHAPTER 2
Frenzy

Everyone at Sam's school was at the park. Sam went in his new yellow car. He wanted to see Mikaela, the most beautiful girl in the school. But Mikaela's boyfriend, Trent, saw Sam first. Trent was good at sport.

'Is that your grandmother's car?' he laughed. He looked down at Sam. 'I remember you. You wanted to be on the school football team. You were terrible!'

'I didn't really want to be on the team,' answered Sam. 'I have better things to do!'

Trent was angry, but Mikaela stopped him.

'Let's go,' she said. She wanted to drive Trent's truck.

'No,' said Trent. 'You're a girl.'

Mikaela was angry. 'But I'm not *your* girl!'

She started to walk away. Sam watched all this from his car. He drove up to Mikaela.

'It's a long way back to town,' he said. 'Can I drive you?'

Mikaela thought about it, and then got into the car.

'Are you new in school?' she asked.

'No … we're in the same class. We were in the same class last year, too.'

'Oh, sorry.'

Suddenly the car stopped and the radio came on. It was a slow love song.

'I didn't do that!' cried Sam. He tried to start the car, but it was dead.

Mikaela got out. 'Let me see,' she said.

As she looked, she told Sam all about cars.

'You know a lot,' he said.

'I learned it from my dad.'

But the car still didn't start.

'I'm going to walk home,' said Mikaela.

Sam just sat and watched as she left. He tried the car one last time and then … yes! It started!

Quickly Sam followed Mikaela. 'Get in!' he called. 'It's working again!'

There was a new song on the radio. This time it was *Please Come Back*.

* * *

Air Force One was in the skies over the USA. Air Force One was the President's jet. There were a lot of important government people on it. They all wanted an answer to the same question – what happened in Qatar?

No one on the jet saw the little CD player. No one saw when it started to move. Long legs came out of it, and then arms and a head. It was the robot, Frenzy. Quietly Frenzy moved through Air Force One. The little robot wanted to find a computer.

* * *

Down in the Pentagon an agent, Maggie Madsen, sat at her computer.

Suddenly she shouted, 'Someone is on the computer on Air Force One! They're looking for something!'

* * *

Frenzy was on the computer on Air Force One. He stopped when he found an old newspaper story, 'Ice Man'. It was about Archibald Witwicky. Suddenly two soldiers saw the little robot. They fired, but he ran away. A minute later Frenzy was just a little CD player again.

* * *

When Air Force One came down, there were soldiers and police everywhere. But no one saw Frenzy. He ran through the dark and into a waiting police car. The robot started to work on a computer in the car.

'They fired their guns at me,' said Frenzy to the driver. 'I didn't get everything, but I have this. We must find this boy.'

On the computer was a photo of Sam Witwicky and Archibald Witwicky's glasses.

CHAPTER 3
The yellow robot

In the night there was a sound from the street. Sam sat up in bed.

'That's my car!' he thought.

Sam ran out of the house. 'No!' he shouted. He started to ride his bike after the car. At the same time, he called the police on his mobile phone. 'Hello, police? Someone is taking my car!'

He followed the car through the streets. Then the car drove over a train line. It drove quickly in front of a train. Sam got off his bike and waited for the train to go. Then he ran across the line to some empty buildings. Suddenly Sam stopped. He could see something in the dark, something yellow. It was standing on two legs. Was it his car? Or was it a giant robot? It fired a light up into the black sky.

'I'm going to die!' Sam thought. He took a photo of the robot with his mobile phone. Then he talked into the phone. 'My name is Sam Witwicky. These are my last words. My car came here without a driver. My car can think! Mom, Dad, I love you.'

Suddenly there was a sound from behind him. Sam turned and saw two big dogs. They both ran at him. 'Oh no!' Sam thought. 'First the car … and now this!'

He turned and ran. But the dogs were fast. Suddenly Sam's car was in front of him. The door opened for him. Was Sam more frightened of the dogs or the car? He didn't know. He just ran.

* * *

In Qatar, Captain Lennox and his men looked at the

photo of the robot from the attack. They wanted to send the photo to the Pentagon. With no radio, Lennox and his men needed a phone. At last they saw some buildings. They started to walk to them, but suddenly something was behind them.

'The robot followed us!' shouted Lennox. 'Run!'

The soldiers fired their guns and ran. People ran out of their houses and fired, too. But the robot didn't stop. It fired missiles from one of its arms. Everything was on fire and buildings started to fall.

At last Lennox found a phone in one of the houses. Quickly he called the Pentagon.

'Help!' he shouted. 'We need jets!'

A minute later, a jet from a different US base was above them.

'Everyone down!' shouted Lennox.

The jet fired missile after missile. The robot didn't die, but it ran away.

'What now?' asked one of the men.

'Now we wait for a helicopter,' Lennox told him. 'We're going back to the USA.'

CHAPTER 4
The open door

The next day Sam was alone in his house. The yellow car came back. It was still without a driver.

Sam was frightened. He ran to his bike and started to ride away. The car followed him. Sam went faster and faster through the busy streets of the town. The car still followed. Soon he was back at the empty buildings again. He heard the sound of a police car and he rode to it.

'Help!' he shouted. 'My car's following me!'

But no one got out. The police car just drove right at Sam. Two big robot arms came out of the front of the car.

'What? What do you want from me?' cried Sam.

The police car started to change in front of him. It changed into a giant black robot with red eyes.

'Are you Sam Witwicky?' it shouted.

Sam didn't answer. He was really frightened now.

'Where are they?' shouted the robot. 'Where are the glasses?'

Sam turned and ran into the street. There was a girl on a bike there. It was Mikaela!

'Go!' shouted Sam.

'What's your problem, Sam?' asked Mikaela angrily. But then she saw the robot!

Suddenly a car drove up to them fast. Sam's yellow car was here. The two teenagers watched as this car changed, too. It had legs, arms, a head, eyes … it was a robot!

The two robots started to fight. Sam and Mikaela watched. Suddenly something ran at them. It was Frenzy, the little robot from the police car.

'Run!' shouted Sam.

Mikaela ran, but the robot was too fast for Sam. Frenzy had him by the legs. The boy and the robot started to fight. Frenzy was quick and strong.

'This is all a bad dream,' thought Sam.

But then Mikaela was behind the robot. She started to hit the robot again and again. Frenzy's head came off. The robot did not move.

'You aren't so strong without a head!' shouted Sam.

The two teenagers turned away, but Frenzy wasn't dead. Behind them the robot changed into a mobile phone and got into Mikaela's bag.

The yellow robot was alone now. It walked slowly to Sam and Mikaela. Sam went to meet it.

'What are you doing?' asked Mikaela.

'I don't think it's going to hurt us,' answered Sam. 'Can you talk?' he asked the robot.

The car radio came on. The sound changed as the robot looked for the right words.

'Do you talk through the radio?' asked Sam.

'That's right!' said the radio.

'Where are you from?' asked Mikaela.

The robot didn't answer. It just changed back into a car and the door opened.

'It wants us to get in,' said Sam.

'And go where?' asked Mikaela.

Sam looked at her. 'I don't want to be too frightened to do this. When we're old, I want to look back and remember this …'

Mikaela just looked at that open door. Then, without saying anything more, the two teenagers got into the car. Before they drove away, they stopped for Mikaela's bag and mobile phone.

* * *

As they sat in the car, Sam and Mikaela talked.

'There's one thing I don't understand,' said Mikaela. 'Why does the robot change into this old yellow car?'

Suddenly the car stopped and the doors opened.

'No! Please, no!' cried Sam, but it was no good. He and Mikaela got out. They watched as the car drove away.

'Why did you say that?' Sam asked Mikaela. 'It heard you! Now it's angry!'

But Sam was wrong. A minute later the car came back. It was still yellow, but now it was a new car. It looked fantastic.

'That's better,' smiled Mikaela.

* * *

When the car stopped, a truck drove up to them. It changed into a giant red and blue robot. The yellow car changed, too. Then three more robots came up.

The biggest robot's face was close to Sam's. 'Are you Sam Witwicky?' he asked.

'Yes,' Sam answered.

'My name is Optimus Prime,' said the robot. 'We are Autobots from the planet Cybertron.'

CHAPTER 5
The Allspark

Optimus told Sam and Mikaela the names of the other robots – Jazz, Ironhide and Ratchet. 'And you already know yellow Bumblebee,' said Optimus Prime.

'Why are you here?' asked Mikaela.

'We are looking for the Allspark,' answered Optimus Prime. 'The Allspark is very special. It can make new robot life. But we must find it before Megatron.'

'Who's Megatron?' asked Sam.

'Megatron is my brother. A long time ago life on our planet was good. But Megatron and his followers, the Decepticons, attacked the other robots. They wanted to be number one on our planet. And so the fight for the Allspark started. More and more robots died. Now our planet is dead. But where is the Allspark? No one knows. Megatron looked for it. He followed it here, to your planet. And Witwicky found him in the ice of the Arctic.'

'Archibald Witwicky?'

'Yes. The robot did not talk or move because it was very cold in the ice. But his computer was still on. It left a picture on Captain Witwicky's glasses. That picture is very important. Without it, we can't find the Allspark.'

Mikaela looked at Sam. 'Please tell me you have those glasses,' she said.

'Megatron wants the Allspark to build new robots,' said Optimus. 'We must stop him. We need those glasses, Sam.'

* * *

The robots changed back into cars and trucks and followed Sam to his house. Sam and Mikaela went quietly into the house and looked for the glasses. Optimus Prime and the other robots waited near the house.

'Where are those glasses?' Sam thought. At last he found them in the kitchen. 'Yes! Here they are.'

At that moment Mikaela thought something moved in her bag. But when she looked, only her mobile phone was there.

Suddenly there was someone at the front door. Sam's dad opened it and saw two government agents in dark clothes.

'Who are you?' asked Mr Witwicky.

'I'm Agent Simmons. We're from Sector 7,' answered the man.

'What's that?'

Agent Simmons didn't answer. 'We're looking for Sam Witwicky,' he said.

Minutes later the two teenagers were in a black car with the government agents.

'Tell me about your car,' Simmons said, smiling.

'Someone took it, but it came back home,' said Sam.

'Yes … *someone* drove it back!' said Mikaela quickly. 'Cars can't drive without drivers!'

Suddenly Simmons stopped smiling. 'What do you know about robots? Robots from a different planet?'

'What? That's just stupid!' said Sam.

Simmons was angry now. 'S7 is a special part of the government. I can do anything. Do you want to see your friends and family again? It is time to talk!'

But just then the car drove right into something – something big – and stopped. Sam looked up and saw the leader of the Autobots.

Sam smiled. 'I want you to meet my friend, Optimus Prime.' The other Autobots were there, too.

'Get out of the car,' said Optimus.

Suddenly government helicopters, trucks and soldiers were everywhere.

The robots were surprised. 'We must not attack the people of this planet,' shouted Optimus to the other Autobots. 'Run!'

The others changed back into cars and trucks and drove away. Optimus had Sam and Mikaela in one big hand. He started running but Sam and Mikaela started to fall …

'This really is the end,' thought Sam.

But then Bumblebee was there. He had Sam and Mikaela in his arms.

'Quick!' shouted Sam. 'The soldiers are coming! Let's go!'

But it was too late. The soldiers were all around them. Now they had Sam, Mikaela … and Bumblebee.

* * *

Optimus Prime was sad. The government agents had one of his Autobots. But he was happy about one thing. He had Archibald Witwicky's glasses.

* * *

At the Pentagon, there was a big problem. First one computer went dead, then the next and the next.

'It's not just our computers! The phones are dead, too. Everything is off, all around the world!' shouted a frightened soldier.

But one man wasn't frightened. His name was Tom Banachek and he was the leader of S7.

A few minutes later the top people from the Pentagon sat and listened to Banachek.

'S7 is a special part of the government,' he said. 'Almost no one knows about us. We started 80 years ago. We look for life from other planets.'

He looked around the room. 'We looked at the photo from Captain Lennox's men in Qatar. We believe that something from a different planet attacked the base.'

* * *

Captain Lennox and his men arrived back in the USA at last. An agent from S7 waited for them.

'We need you and your team to come with us right now,' he said. 'Let's go.'

* * *

Sam and Mikaela were in a government helicopter. Under them was the blue water of the Hoover Dam.

Maggie Madsen sat opposite the teenagers. She was here because she saw the attack on the computers.

'Why are you here?' she asked Sam.

'I bought a car,' he answered. 'Then I learned that it was a robot from another planet.'

CHAPTER 6
The Ice Man

Sam, Mikaela and Maggie followed Tom Banachek and Agent Simmons into a big room inside the Hoover Dam. There was a big robot there – much bigger than Bumblebee. It didn't move because it was under ice.

'Your grandfather found this 80 years ago in the Arctic, Sam. We keep it here,' said Simmons. 'We call it the Ice Man.'

But Sam knew the robot's true name. 'That's Megatron,' he said. 'His followers are the Decepticons.'

Captain Lennox was there, too. He looked up at the robot. 'Why are they here on Earth?'

'They're looking for something,' said Sam. 'They call it the Allspark.' Sam looked at the S7 agents. 'Do you already know about the Allspark?'

Banachek just said, 'Follow me.'

* * *

The Allspark was in a special room.

'I can't believe it's here, in the same place as Megatron,' said Sam.

'Why is the Allspark so special?' asked Maggie. 'What can it do?'

Agent Simmons had a mobile phone in his hand. 'Watch.'

He put the phone near the Allspark. The mobile phone started moving. Six legs came out of it. It started running around. It tried to attack the people in the room.

'The Allspark can do that to anything – phones, radios, computers, CD players … ' said Banachek.

Sam was really frightened. 'Megatron gets that thing, and everyone on the planet is going to die,' he said.

The Decepticons' little robot, Frenzy, was out of Mikaela's bag now. He listened in the dark to Banachek's words. Then he called the other Decepticons, 'Megatron is here. And the Allspark is here, too. Come quickly!'

Starscream, the jet; Barricade, the police car; Bonecrusher, the truck; and Blackout, the helicopter, all started moving to the Hoover Dam. The first one to arrive was Starscream. He started firing at the soldiers.

Inside the building Frenzy was on the computers. It was warm in Megatron's big room now. Soon the ice around the big robot started to fall off. Frenzy laughed.

'The Ice Man is waking up!' he shouted.

* * *

In a different room, soldiers started getting ready for the fight with the Decepticons. Sam went up to Agent Simmons.

'Take me to my car,' he said.

'No, I can't do that,' shouted Simmons.

But then Simmons stopped. There was a gun at his head. It was Captain Lennox's gun.

'Take him to the car,' Lennox said.

When Sam saw Bumblebee, there were soldiers with guns all around the robot.

'Stop!' shouted Sam at the soldiers. 'What are you doing?'

The robot was angry and frightened, but he didn't fire at the soldiers.

Sam looked up. 'Listen to me, Bumblebee. The Decepticons are coming. The Allspark is here.'

'We are going to die if we stay here,' said Captain Lennox. 'Mission City isn't far away. We must take the Allspark there. Let's go!'

Sam and Mikaela went in Bumblebee, with the Allspark in the back. Captain Lennox and his men followed in a truck.

* * *

In another part of the building, Megatron woke up at last. His red eyes looked around.

'I AM MEGATRON!' he shouted. 'Get the Allspark!'

* * *

As they drove to the city, Sam saw a truck and three cars in front of them.

'That's Optimus. And there's Jazz and Ironhide. Ratchet is here, too!' cried Sam, happily. 'They used the glasses and found us!'

When they saw Bumblebee, the other Autobots turned and followed. They were near the city now.

'The last fight for the Allspark is going to happen here,' thought Sam.

CHAPTER 7
The last fight

On the streets of the city, Sam and Mikaela waited with the Autobots and Lennox's men. There was a jet in the sky over the city.

'It's here to help us!' cried Lennox.

'No!' shouted Ironhide. 'That's Starscream!'

Everyone started running as the Decepticon fired its first missiles. Everything went white around Sam. When he opened his eyes, he saw Bumblebee with fire all around him. The Autobot didn't look good.

'He can't walk!' shouted Mikaela. 'I think he's dying.'

'I'm not going to leave you,' Sam told Bumblebee. But Bumblebee had the Allspark in his hand. He gave it to Sam.

Lennox and his men ran to them. 'The Autobots and the Decepticons are fighting,' he said. 'Jazz is dead.'

There was a tall, white building behind them. Lennox said, 'Sam, take the Allspark to the top of that white building. A government helicopter is coming soon. Give them the Allspark.'

Mikaela went up to Sam. 'I just want you to know,' she said. 'We were right to get into the car.'

Sam ran for his life.

'Megatron is here!' shouted Optimus Prime.

The giant Decepticon was on top of a building. 'The people of this planet are nothing!' he shouted. 'They're all going to die and you, brother, are going to die with them.'

The fight between the two brothers started. Megatron pushed Optimus hard against the building and Optimus was down.

Megatron was behind Sam now. Sam was very tired, but he didn't stop running. He ran into the white building.

'Where are you, boy?' Megatron screamed.

'Don't stop!' Sam thought as he ran. 'You're near the top now!'

At last Sam was on top of the building with the Allspark in his hands. But where was the helicopter? Then he saw it at last.

Sam shouted, 'Over here! I've got the Allspark!'

But it was too late. Megatron found him. The robot fired a missile at the helicopter. BOOM!

'Now what can I do?' Sam thought. There was nowhere to go.

'Give me the Allspark,' said the Decepticon. 'Then you can live.'

Sam was really frightened, but he answered, 'No way!'

'How stupid!' cried Megatron. He fired and Sam started falling down, down, down . . .

But then big hands closed around him. 'I've got you!' said Optimus Prime. The big robot put Sam down carefully in the street.

'At the end of today only one brother can live,' said Optimus. 'Megatron must not have the Allspark. If I die, push the Allspark into my body. Then the Allspark dies with me.'

Optimus walked up to Megatron. Sam looked up at the two robots. They were ready for their last fight.

'It's just you and me, Megatron,' said Optimus.

'No! It's just ME, Prime!'

The fight started.

* * *

The government jets were over the city now. They started firing missiles at the Decepticons.

'Attack!' shouted Captain Lennox.

* * *

But things did not look so good for Optimus Prime. He was down after another hit from Megatron.

'Sam, quick!' cried Optimus. 'Push the Allspark into my body!'

But Sam had a different idea. He quickly turned and pushed the Allspark into Megatron's body.

There was a very loud, very high scream. Then at last Megatron was quiet and the red eyes closed.

Optimus looked down at Megatron's dead body. 'Goodbye, brother,' he said quietly.

* * *

For Sam and Mikaela a new life started. They were very happy together, and Sam had the best yellow car in the world. Without the Allspark, the other Autobots were alone. They decided to stay on this planet. They are still here. Maybe that truck on your street is an Autobot. Maybe the jet in the sky is one. No one knows about them, but they are our friends. This is their home now.

FACT FILE

It started with a toy ...

We all know that Transformers are cars that change into robots. But when and where did the idea start?

Robot or truck?

In 1984 the toymakers, Hasbro, introduced their new toys – cars, trucks and jets which changed into robots. The idea for these toys came from Japan. Robots were already popular toys there.

Hasbro immediately liked the idea and they gave each robot a personality. Writers wrote a story for each toy. The story was about the planet Cybertron. Hasbro called the toys 'Transformers'.

Early Transformers toys

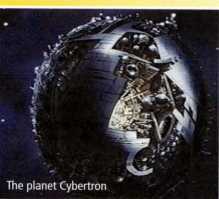

The planet Cybertron

Here to stay

Children loved the new toys and they also loved the stories. They really cared about their robots. The Transformers were here to stay. 300 million toys later, they are one of the most popular toys of all time.

Books, TV and film

But the story of the Transformers did not stop at the toys. Over the next twenty years there were comic books and TV shows. In 1986 there was a film – *Transformers: The Movie*. The latest film in 2007 introduced new teenagers to the world of the Transformers. Where does the story go from here?

Prime fact

In the 1986 film *Transformers: The Movie*, Optimus Prime dies. Many people were not happy about this!

Q: How long does it take to design a new Transformers toy and get it into the shops?

A: More than two years.

What do you think?
What toys did you play with when you were a child? What was your favourite toy? Why did you like it?

Do you know these words?
You can use a dictionary.
**introduce   toy/s   popular
personality   TV show/s   design**

FACT FILE

TRANSFORMERS

The 2007 film *Transformers* was a big hit, thanks to some famous names and some new young stars. Let's meet them ...

Steven Spielberg was one of the producers of the film. He loved the idea of a Transformers film. Years ago he bought the toys – not for his children, but for him! But this film is not only about the robots. For Spielberg, this film is really about 'a boy and his car'.

Michael Bay was the director of the film. He is famous for his action films. There are many stunts in the film – only the robots are computer-generated. The film was expensive to make – $150 million – but it was a big hit and MTV's best film in 2008.

Did you know?

In the comic books, Bumblebee was a yellow Volkswagen Beetle, but in the film he changes into a Chevrolet Camaro.

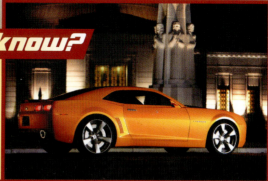

Shia Laboeuf (Sam Witwicky) was born in 1986 in Los Angeles, USA. As a boy, Shia loved the Transformers toys – so he was very happy to play Sam. In the film he did his own stunts. *Transformers* was one of Shia's first films. He is now a very busy young star. In 2008 he starred in Spielberg's *Indiana Jones and the Kingdom of the Crystal Skull*.

Megan Fox (Mikaela Banes) was also born in 1986, in Tennessee, USA. Megan moved to Florida when she was 10. She started acting when she was 13. Before *Transformers*, Megan was a television star. In the film she did a lot of running. When she met Michael Bay, he had one important question for her: 'Can you run fast?'

What do you think?
Who are your favourite film stars?
What films are they in?

What do these words mean?
You can use a dictionary.
producer   toy/s   director   action
stunt/s   computer-generated   acting

FACT FILE

Robot World

Say the word 'robot' and most people think of films like *Transformers* and *Star Wars*. But there are many working robots in the world today …

 Robots can do some jobs faster and better than people. There are many robots in factories. Car factories often use big robot arms to make cars.

Robots can visit dangerous places that people cannot. Scientists are developing robots which can go to the Arctic. Robots can also go to other planets. The first of these robots was the *Sojourner Rover*. It went to Mars in 1997.

Sojourner Rover

Asimo

When people visit the Honda building in Tokyo, a robot meets them. The robot's name is Asimo and it is 130 cm tall. It can talk, walk and climb stairs. The robot can answer to its name and knows about 10 different faces. Honda scientists worked for 20 years to develop Asimo. In the future, scientists may use robots like Asimo to care for people, or do dangerous jobs such as fighting fires.

Some robots can already play chess better than people. Other robots can 'read' people's faces – they 'know' when people are angry or happy. But are robots ever going to have their own thoughts? And what are they going to think about us?

What do you think?
Is it important to develop new robots?
What jobs would you like a robot to do?

What do these words mean?
You can use a dictionary.
factory / factories   dangerous
scientist/s   develop   chess

SELF-STUDY ACTIVITIES

CHAPTERS 1-2

Before you read

1 Read 'People and Places' on pages 4–5. Answer these questions.
   a) Who wants a car?
   b) Who is Sam in love with?
   c) Who is the leader of the Autobots?
   d) Who can change into a yellow car?
   e) Who is very good with computers?
   f) What is the Pentagon?

2 Complete the sentences with these words.
   attack   leader   planet   scream   giant
   a) A … goes round the sun.
   b) Megatron is the … of the Decepticons.
   c) Some people … when they are frightened.
   d) That big dog is going to … us. Run!
   e) The … robot was taller than a building.

3 Match the two columns.
   a) She **got out** of the car   i) have a **robot** in their house.
   b) The boy was frightened because   ii) when I was a child.
   c) England's **government** is   iii) in London.
   d) I didn't like wearing **glasses**   iv) the man had a **gun**.
   e) One day everyone will   v) and it drove away.

After you read

4 Are these sentences true or false? Correct the false sentences.
   a) The helicopter at the base in Qatar changes into a giant robot.
   b) Sam Witwicky shows the class his grandfather's glasses.
   c) Mr Witwicky buys his son a car for five thousand dollars.
   d) Mikaela is a good friend of Sam's.
   e) Maggie Madsen works on Air Force One.
   f) Frenzy wants to know more about Archibald Witwicky.
   g) When Air Force One comes down, the police find Frenzy.

5 Choose the correct words.
  a) People *believed / didn't believe* Archibald Witwicky's story.
  b) Sam wants to *buy / sell* some glasses.
  c) Sam is *good / bad* at sports.
  d) Mikaela gets into Sam's new *truck / car*.
  e) The robot, Frenzy, changes into a *jet / CD player*.

CHAPTERS 3-4

Before you read
  6 What do you think?
  a) Who is the 'Ice Man' in the newspaper story?
  b) What is special about Sam's car?
  c) Are Sam and Mikaela going to be friends?

After you read
  7 Put these parts of the story in order.
  a) The police car changes into a black robot.
  b) The yellow robot fights the black robot.
  c) Sam and Mikaela meet the other Autobots.
  d) Sam meets Mikaela in the street.
  e) The old yellow car changes into a new car.
  f) Sam's car follows him.
  g) Mikaela hits Frenzy.

  8 Who is speaking?
  a) 'Hello, police? Someone is taking my car!'
  b) 'These are my last words.'
  c) 'We need jets!'
  d) 'Where are the glasses?'
  e) 'What's your problem, Sam?'
  f) 'When we're old. I want to look back and remember this …'
  g) 'We are Autobots from the planet Cybertron.'

SELF-STUDY ACTIVITIES

CHAPTERS 5-7

Before you read

9 Complete the sentences with these words. You can use a dictionary.

agent   fight   missiles   push

a) An … usually works for a government.
b) … is the opposite of *pull*.
c) A fighter jet has a lot of … .
d) 'Don't …!' the teacher told the two boys.

After you read

10 Answer the questions.

a) What can make new robot life?
b) Why didn't Megatron talk when Archibald found him?
c) Who does Agent Simmons work for?
d) Who do the soldiers have?
e) Where do the agents take Sam and Mikaela?

11 Complete the sentences with these names.

Frenzy   Mikaela   Megatron   Bumblebee   Optimus   Sam

a) … is the 'Ice Man'.
b) … calls the Decepticons.
c) … can't walk after a missile hits him.
d) … pushes the Allspark into Megatron's body.
e) … says, 'Goodbye, brother.'
f) … is happy with Sam.

12 What do you think?

a) Are the Autobots going to be happy in their new home? Why / Why not?
b) What will the Decepticons do?
c) Will Sam sell his car?

13 What do you think?
Who did you like best in the story? Who did you not like?